D0872151

GHOST
of chance

GHOST of chance

wILLIam S. BURROUGHS

HIGH RISK BOOKS

NEW YORK / LONDON

This is a work of fiction. Names, characters, places and incidents are either the product of the author's imagination or are used fictitiously. Any resemblance to actual events or persons, living or dead, is entirely coincidental.

The right of William S. Burroughs to be acknowledged as author of this work has been asserted by him in accordance with the Copyright, Designs and Patents Act 1988

A catalogue record for this book can be obtained from the British Library on request

Library of Congress Catalog Card Number: 95-68012

Copyright © 1991 by William S. Burroughs

All rights reserved under the International and Pan-American Copyright Conventions

First published in 1991 as a limited edition by the Library Fellows of the Whitney Museum of American Art

This edition first published in 1995 by
Serpent's Tail,
4 Blackstock Mews, London N4,
and 180 Varick Street, 10th floor, New York, NY 10014

Typeset by CentraCet Limited, Cambridge
Printed in Finland by Werner Söderström Oy

CAPTAIN MISSION STRAPPED on his double-barreled flintlock, which he kept loaded with shot charges, and thrust a scabbarded cutlass under his belt. He picked up his staff and walked out through the settlement, stopping here and there to talk to the settlers.

They had found an excellent red clay for bricks and were constructing two-story dwellings with second-story balconies supported by heavy hardwood pillars. These buildings had been joined to form a tier, with the dining and kitchen areas in the two downstairs rooms and the sleeping and dressing areas upstairs. The balconies were connected and were used for sleeping hammocks and pallets. These structures faced the sea, and steps led down to the bay, where a number of boats were moored.

*

THE WORD FOR 'lemur' meant 'ghost' in the native language. There were taboos against the killing of ghosts, and Mission had imposed an Article that prohibited killing them, on penalty of expulsion from the settlement. If any crime deserved the death penalty, also prohibited under the Articles, then this was that crime.

He was seeking a different lemur species, described by a native informant as much bigger—like a calf, or a little cow.

'Where are the big ghosts?'

The native gestured vaguely inland. 'You must be careful of the evil Lizard-Who-Changes-Color. If you fall under its spell, you too will change color. You too will turn black with anger, and green with fear, and red with sex . . .'

'Well, what is so wrong with that?'

'In a year you will die. The colors will devour your skin and flesh.'

'You were talking about a big ghost. Bigger than a goat . . . Where are they to be found?'

'When you hear Chebahaka, Man-in-the-Trees, then Big One not there. Her cannot be where noise is.'

'Her?'

'Her. He. For Big Ghost is same.'

'So. He is where Man-in-the-Trees isn't?'

'No. He is there when Man-in-the-Trees is silent.'

This occurred at dawn and sunset.

*

MISSION WAS HEADING inland, up a steep path that leveled off at five hundred feet above the sea. He stopped, leaning on his staff, and looked back. The steep climb had not touched his breath or brought sweat to his face. He saw the settlement, the freshly molded red bricks and thatch already timeless as houses in a fairyland. He could see the shadows that lay under the pier, the lurking fish, the clear blue water of the bay, the rocks and foliage, all floating in a limpid, frameless painting.

Silence descended like a shroud that would crumble to dust when he moved. Now a cat's-paw of wind frisked across the bay and up through the ferns and leaves, bringing to his face a breath of Panic. Little ghost paws rippled up his spine, stirring the hairs at the nape of his neck, where the death center flares briefly when a mortal dies.

3

Captain Mission did not fear Panic, the sudden, intolerable knowing that everything is alive. He was himself an emissary of Panic, of the knowledge that man fears above all else: the truth of his origin. It's so close. Just wipe away the words and look.

He moved through giant ferns and creepers in green shade without need of his cutlass, and stopped on the edge of a clearing. A moment of arrested motion, then a bush, a stone, a log moved, as a tribe of ring-tailed cat lemurs appeared, parading back and forth around each other, tails quivering above their heads. Then *whisk*—they were gone, drawing the space where they had been away with them. In the distance he could hear the cries of the sifaka lemur the natives called Chebahaka, Man-in-the-Trees.

With a quick motion he caught a grasshopper and knelt by a moss-covered log. A tiny face with round eyes and large trembling ears peered at him nervously. He held out the grasshopper, and the little mouse lemur fell upon it with chirping squeaks of delight, holding it in his small paws and nibbling quickly with his tiny needle teeth.

Mission moved toward the sound, which grew louder and louder. The Chebahakas saw him now, and they let out a concerted shriek that pierced his eardrums. Then suddenly the sound stopped, with an impact that threw him to the ground. He lay for some minutes in a half-faint, watching the gray shapes swing away through the trees.

Slowly he rose to his feet, leaning on his staff. Before him stood an ancient stone structure, overgrown with creepers and green with moss. He stepped through an archway, stone slabs under his feet. A large snake, of a glistening bright green, glided down the steps leading to an underground room. Cautiously he descended. At the far end of the room an arch opened to admit the afternoon light, and he could see the stone walls and ceiling.

In the corner of the second room was an animal that looked like a small gorilla or a chimpanzee. This surprised him, since he had been told that there

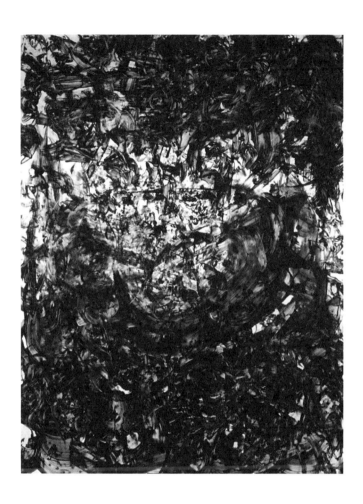

were no true monkeys on the island. The creature was completely motionless, and black, as if formed out of darkness. He saw also a large pig creature of a light pink color, lolling on its side against the wall to his right.

Then, directly in front of him, he saw an animal that looked at first like a small deer. The animal came to his outstretched hand, and he saw that it had no horns. Its snout was long, and he glimpsed sharp teeth shaped like little scimitars. The long thin legs ended in cablelike fingers. The ears were large, flaring forward, the eyes limpid amber, in which the pupil floated like a glittering jewel, changing color with shifts of the light: obsidian, emerald, ruby, opal, amethyst, diamond.

Slowly the animal raised one paw and touched his face, stirring memories of the ancient betrayal. Tears streaming down his face, he stroked the animal's head. He knew he must get back to the settlement before dark. There is always something a man must do in time. For the deer ghost there was no time.

FASTER AND FASTER downhill, tearing his clothing on rocks and thorny vines, and by dusk he was back at the settlement. He knew at once that he was too late, that something was horribly wrong. No one would meet his eye. Then he saw Bradley Martin, standing over a dying lemur.

Mission could see that the lemur had been

5

shot through the body. He felt a concentration of rage, like a hot red wave, but there was no reciprocal anger in Martin.

'Why?' Mission choked out.

'Stole my mango,' Martin muttered insolently.

Mission's hand flew to the butt of his pistol.

Martin laughed. 'You would violate your own Article, Captain?'

'No. But I will remind you of Article Twenty-Three: If two parties have a disagreement that cannot be settled, then the rule of the duel is applicable.'

'Aye, but I have the right to refuse your challenge, and I do.'

Martin was an indifferent swordsman and a poor pistol shot.

'Then you must leave Libertatia, this very night, before the sun shall set. You have no more than an hour.'

Without a word, Martin turned away and walked off in the direction of his dwelling. Mission covered the dead lemur with a tarpaulin, intending to take the body into the jungle and bury it the following morning.

IN HIS QUARTERS Mission was suddenly overcome by a paralyzing fatigue. He knew that he should follow Martin and settle the matter, but—as Martin had said—his own Articles . . . He lay down and fell immediately into a deep sleep. He dreamed that there were dead lemurs scattered through the settlement, and woke up at dawn with tears streaming down his face.

MISSION DRESSED AND went out to get the dead lemur, but the lemur and the tarpaulin were both gone. With blinding clarity he understood why Martin had shot the lemur, and what he intended to do: he would go to the natives and say that the settlers were killing the lemurs and that, when he objected, they turned on him and he had barely escaped with his life. Lemurs were sacred to the natives in the area, and there was the danger of bloody reprisal.

Mission blamed himself bitterly for allowing Martin to escape. No use to go looking for him now. The damage was already done, and the natives would never believe Mission's denials.[1]

*

1. Consider the inexorable logic of the Big Lie. If a man has a consuming love for cats and dedicates himself to the protection of cats, you have only to accuse him of killing and mistreating cats. Your lie will have the unmistakable ring of truth, whereas his outraged denials will reek of falsehood and evasion.

Those who have heard voices from the nondominant brain hemisphere remark on the absolute authority of the voice. They know they are hearing the Truth. The fact that no evidence is adduced and that the voice may be talking utter nonsense is irrelevant. This is what Truth *is*. And Truth has nothing to do with *facts*. Those who manipulate Truth to their advantage, the people of the Big Lie, are careful to shun facts. In fact nothing is more deeply offensive to such people than the concept of fact. To adduce fact in

BIG BEN STRIKES the hour. In a muted, ghostly room, the custodians of the future convene. Keeper of the Board Books: Mektoub, it is written. And they don't want it changed.

'If three hundred men—then three thousand, thirty thousand. It could spread everywhere. It must be stopped *now*.'

'Our man Martin is on target. Quite reliable.'

A woman leans slightly forward. An arresting face of timeless beauty and evil, an evil that stops the breath like a deadly gas. The chairman covers his face with a handkerchief.

She speaks in a cold, brittle voice, each word a chip of obsidian: 'There is a more significant danger. I refer to Captain Mission's unwholesome concern with *lemurs*.'

The word slithers out of her mouth writhing with hatred.

THERE ARE NO further repercussions from the incident with Martin. But Mission does not slacken his precautions. He can feel Martin out there waiting

---

your defense is to rule yourself out of court.

In a prerecorded and therefore totally predictable universe, the blackest sin is to tamper with the prerecordings, which could result in altering the prerecorded future. Captain Mission was guilty of this sin. He threatened to demonstrate for all to see that three hundred souls can coexist in relative harmony with each other, with their neighbors, and with the ecosphere of flora and fauna.

his time with the cold reptilian patience of the perfect agent.

He had underestimated Martin from the beginning by not seeing him. Martin had the capacity to create a lack of interest in himself.[2] Even his position was ambiguous, something between a petty officer and a member of the crew. But since there were no petty officers, he occupied an empty space. And he made no attempt to fill it. When told to do something he did it quickly and efficiently. Yet he made no attempt to make himself useful.

Since Mission found contact with Martin vaguely disagreeable, he asked him to do less and less. Mission was displeased that Martin chose to join the settlers, but he did his share of the work and bothered no one. When he was not working he would simply sit, his face as empty as a plate. He was a large, sloppy man with a round pasty face and yellow hair. His eyes were dull and cold like lead.

Mission *saw* Martin for the first time as they confronted each other over the dying lemur. And what he saw inspired in him a deadly, implacable hatred.

He sees Martin as the paid servant of everything he detests. No quarter, no compromise is possible. This is war to extermination.

*

2. If you wish to conceal anything, you have only to create a lack of interest in the place where it is hidden.

MISSION HAD SMOKED opium and hashish and had used a drug called *yagé* by the Indians of South America. There must, he decided, be a special drug peculiar to this huge island, where there were so many creatures and plants not found anywhere else. After some inquiries, he found that such a drug did exist: it was extracted from a parasitic fungus that grew only on a certain spiny plant found in the arid regions of the south.

The drug was called *indri*, which meant 'look there' in the native language. For five gold florins he obtained a small supply from a friendly native. The drug was in the form of greenish-yellow crystals. The man, whose name was Babuchi, showed him exactly how much to take and cautioned him against taking any more.

'Many take *indri* and see nothing different. Then they take more and see too much different.'

'Is this a day drug or a night drug?'

'Best at dawn and twilight.'

Mission calculated an hour till sundown— enough time to reach his jungle camp.

'How long does it take to work?'

'Very quick.'

MISSION SET OUT walking rapidly. Half an hour later, he took a small amount of the crystals with a sip of water from his goatskin water-bag. In a few minutes he experienced a shift of vision, as if his eyes were moving on separate pivots, and for the first time he saw Lizard-Who-Changes-Color. It was quite large, about two feet in length, and difficult to see, not because it took on the colors of its surroundings, but because it was absolutely motionless. He moved closer to the lizard, which brought one eye to bear on him and turned black with rage. Evidently Lizard-Who-Changes-Color did not like to be seen. Its colors subsided, to a neutral orange-yellow mottled with brown. And there was a gurkha lizard on a limb, as if carved from the bark. It winked a golden eye at Mission.

Despite the need for vigilance, Mission was spending more and more time in the jungle with his lemurs. He had converted the ancient stone structure he had found into a dwelling. It was completely enveloped by the roots of a huge bulbous tree, as if held in a giant hand. The open arch in the second room was festooned with roots. There was a paved floor. He had covered the entrance with mosquito netting and arranged a pallet on the floor. Brushing the floor, he was surprised to find few insects, certainly no venomous varieties. The stone steps were worn smooth as if with the passage of many feet, perhaps not human feet.

Since his first encounter he had located a troop of the larger lemurs. These lemurs were too big and heavy to be comfortable in arboreal conditions and lived mostly on the land, in an area of grass and scrub where the forest thinned out, a mile from his campsite. Ideal grazing land, Mission realized with a shudder. The creatures were trusting and gentle and open to human affection.

11

Mission hurried on. He wanted to reach the ancient stone structure before twilight, and he hoped his special lemur would be there. He often slept with the lemur beside him on his pallet and had named the creature Ghost.

As Mission walked up, Ghost gave a little chittering cry of welcome. Mission took off his boots and hung his outer garment on wooden pegs driven into chinks in the stone wall. The only furniture was a wall-mounted table of rough-hewn planks supported on two legs, with an ink pot, quill pens, and parchment. In one corner were a small water keg with a spigot, some cooking utensils, an ax, a saw, hammers, a musket. Powder and shot were kept in the footlocker.

12

MISSION SAT AT the wooden table beside his phantom, his Ghost, contemplating the mystery of the stone structure. Who could have built it?

Who?

He poses the question in hieroglyphs . . . a feather . . . He chooses a quill pen. Water . . . the clear water under the pier. A book . . . an old illustrated book with gilt edges. *The Ghost Lemurs of Madagascar*. Feather . . . a gull diving for garbage . . . the wakes of many ships in many places. A feather of the Great Bird that lived here once, and the Sacred Lake two days' walk east, where every year a heifer is sacrificed to the Sacred Crocodile. Still, Mission wonders if there are other, similar structures on the island . . .

Where?

A loaf of bread . . . water . . . a jar . . . a goose tied to a stake. Looking from one end of the island to the other, through the eyes of Lizard-Who-Changes-Color. Mission doesn't know why he is appalled by the questions that lunge into his mind, but he is satisfied, almost, to be appalled.

When?

A reed . . . a loaf of bread . . . A bird wheels in the sky. A woman plucks feathers from a fowl, takes a loaf of bread from an adobe oven. The split between the wild, the timeless, the free, and the tame, the time-bound, the tethered, like the tethered goose that will forever resent its bondage.

The structure that has already begun to **13** obsess Mission could have been built at only one time, before the Split widened to a Chasm.

The concept of a question is reed and water. The question mark fades into reeds and water. The question does not exist.

Strange creatures are fitting stones together. Mission can't see them clearly, only their hands, like gray ropes. He senses the immense difficulty of an unaccustomed task. The stones are too heavy for these creatures' hands and bodies. Yet for some reason they must build this structure.

Why?

There is no reason why.

*

GHOST STIRRED BESIDE Mission and belched a sweet scent of tamarind fruit. Despite Babuchi's warning, Captain Mission knew he must learn more.

He lit a candle and poured a reckless dose of *indri* crystals into his hand; he downed them with a cup of water. Almost immediately, he remembered the dream gorilla in the basement room, the strange pig creature he had seen, and then the gentle deer lemur.

Mission lay down by his Ghost. He wasn't sure he wanted to see what the *indri* would show him; already he knew that what he saw would be sad beyond endurance. He looked out through tree roots as night sopped up the remaining light like a vast black sponge.

He lay there in the gray light, his arm around his lemur. The animal snuggled closer and put a paw up to his face. Tiny mouse lemurs stole out of the roots and niches and holes in the ancient tree and frisked around the room, falling on insects with little squeals. Their tails twitched above their heads; their great flaring ears, thin as paper, quivered to every sound as their wide, limpid eyes swept the walls and floors for insects. They had been doing this for millions of years. The twitching tail, the trembling ears mark the passage of centuries.

As the light drained into the sponge of night, Mission could see for miles in every direction: the coastal rain forests, the mountains and scrub of the interior, the arid southern regions where the lemurs were frisking in the tall, spiny *Didierea* cactus. They gambol, leap, and whisk away into the remote past before the arrival of man on this island, before the appearance of man on earth, before the beginning of time.

AN OLD PICTURE book with gilt-edged etchings, onion paper over each picture . . . *The Ghost Lemurs of Madagascar* in gold script. Giant ferns and palms, bulbous tamarind trees, vines and bushes. In a corner of the picture is a huge bird, ten feet high, a plump, dowdy, helpless bird, obviously flightless. This bird tells one that here is a time pocket. There can be no predators in this forest, no large cats. In the middle of the picture is a ring-tailed lemur on a branch, looking straight out at the viewer. Now more lemurs appear, as in a puzzle . . .

15

The Lemur People are older than Homo Sap, much older. They date back one hundred sixty million years, to the time when Madagascar split off from the mainland of Africa. Their way of thinking and feeling is basically different from ours, not oriented toward time and sequence and causality. They find these concepts repugnant and difficult to understand.

One might think that a species that leaves no fossil record is gone forever, but Big Picture, the history of life on earth, is there for anyone to read. Mountain landmasses and jungles glide past, some slowing, some accelerating, vast rivers of land on the move or stagnating in wide deltas, whirlpools of land like saws splitting off islands, a great fissure, the landmasses rubbing against each other, then splitting, flying apart, faster and faster . . . slowing down to the great red island, with its deserts and rain forests, scrub mountains and lakes, its unique animals and plants, and the absence of predators or venomous reptiles, a vast sanctuary for the lemurs and for the delicate spirits that breathe through them, the glint in the jeweled eyes of a tree frog.

When attached to Africa, Madagascar was the ultimate landmass, sticking out like a disorderly tumor cut by a rift of future contours, this long rift like a vast indentation, like the cleft that divides the human body. The rift was a mile across in places, and in others narrowed to a few hundred feet. It was an area of explosive change and contrast, swept by violent electrical storms, incredibly fertile in places, entirely barren in others.

The People of the Cleft, formulated by chaos and accelerated time, flash through a hundred sixty million years to the Split. Which side are you on? Too late to change now. Separated by a curtain of fire. Like a vast festive ship launched with fireworks, the great red island moved majestically out to sea, leaving a gaping wound in the earth's side, bleeding lava, and spurting noxious gases. It has lain moored in enchanted calm for a hundred sixty million years.

Time is a human affliction; not a human invention but a prison. So what is the meaning of one

hundred sixty million years without time? And what does time mean to foraging lemurs? No predators here, not much to fear. They have opposing thumbs but do not fashion tools; they have no need for tools. They are untouched by the evil that flows in and fills Homo Sap as he picks up a weapon—now *he* has the advantage. A terrible gloating feeling comes from knowing you've *got it!*

Beauty is always doomed. 'The evil and armed draw near.' Homo Sap with his weapons, his time, his insatiable greed, and ignorance so hideous it can never see its own face.

Man was born in time. He lives and dies in time. Wherever he goes, he takes time with him and imposes time.

17

CAPTAIN MISSION WAS drifting out faster and faster, caught in a vast undertow of time. 'Out, and under, and out, and out,' a voice repeated in his head.[3]

Mission knows the stone temple is the entrance to the biological Garden of Lost Chances. Pay and enter. He feels an impact of sadness that stops his breath, a catching, tearing grief. This grief can kill. He is beginning to learn the coinage here.

He remembers the pink pig creature, lost in

3. Erase the concept of a question from your mind. The Egyptian glyph is a reed or feather and water. Who? The water the feather the book. Wipe it out with the squawking goose of where and the bread of when, fading into a great, extinct, flightless bird in a swampy pool.

passive weakness, slumped hopelessly against the wall, and the black simian against the far wall by the entrance, very still and very black, a blackness that glows. And the gentle deer lemur, extinct for two thousand years, the Ghost that shares his pallet. He moves forward through the roots that trail from the ancient stone arch. Somehow the black monkey creature is in front of him, and he looks into its eyes, completely black. It is singing a black song, a harsh melody of a blackness too pure to survive in time. It is only compromise that survives; that is why Homo Sap is such a muddled, unsightly creature, precariously and hysterically defending a position that he knows is hopelessly compromised.

18　　　　　Mission moves through a black tunnel, which opens onto a series of dioramas: The last deer lemur falls to a hunter's arrow. Passenger pigeons rain from the trees to salvos of gunfire and plump down on the plates of fat bankers and politicians with their gold watch chains and gold fillings. The humans belch out the last passenger pigeon. The last Tasmanian wolf limps through a blue twilight, one leg shattered by a hunter's bullet. As do the almosts, the might-have-beens who had one chance in a billion and lost.[4]

　　　　　Observe the observer observed.

4. When we see the planet as an organism, it is obvious who the enemies of the planet are. Their name is legion. They dominate and populate the planet. 'The deceived and the deceivers who are themselves deceived.' Did Homo Sap think other animals were there just for him to *eat*? Apparently. Bulldozers are destroying

the rain forests, the cowering lemurs and flying foxes, the singing Kloss's gibbons, which produce the most beautiful and variegated music of any land animal, and the gliding colugo lemurs, which are helpless on the ground. All going, to make way for more and more devalued human stock, with less and less wild spark, the priceless ingredient—energy into matter. A vast mud-slide of soulless sludge.

||

TROUBLE WAS ON the way. Captain Mission could feel it. He had received a report from a native informant, reliable in the past, that a joint French and English expeditionary force was on the way to attack his free pirate settlement, Libertatia, on the west coast of Madagascar. Preferring a sea battle, on waters he knew well, to an attempt to defend a land position on four fronts, he set about outfitting three ships. Before sailing, he paid a visit to the entrance of the Museum of Lost Species.

IN THE MORNING, Ghost had rubbed against him, mewling plaintively. *He knows I am leaving him.* Mission walked rapidly away and turned; Ghost was still there looking after him, waiting.

*

AFTER THREE DAYS at sea, with no sign of an expeditionary force and no word from any of the native crews he stopped and questioned, Mission realized that the siege story was a trick to lure him away from the settlement, and he turned back. Delayed by head winds, he did not arrive at Libertatia for eight days.

From the harbor he saw that the settlement was now a burnt-out ruin, with nothing left but the smell of ashes and death. Mission headed inland, a sick fear in his stomach. He made his way past the carnage on the land and through the jungle to the ancient structure.

THE ARCH HAS been blown to fragments by an explosive charge, the torn roots like broken hands spilling stone and rubble. Mission hears a faint chittering cry: Ghost is pinned under a heavy stone. He pries the stone aside and gathers the dying lemur in his arms, knowing that Ghost has been there waiting for him. The lemur puts a slow paw up to his face with a sad, weak cry. The paw drops. Mission knows that a chance that occurs only once in a hundred sixty million years has been lost forever.

THE ENTRANCE . . . an old film . . . dim, grainy explosive charge . . . plaintive paw up to his face . . . He knows I am a hundred sixty million years away . . . Torn roots like broken hands . . . a sad, weak cry.

21

This grief can kill, but Captain Mission is a soldier. He will not surrender to the enemy. With an agonizing wrench his grief forms an imprecation.[5]

He transmutes his grief into an incandescent blaze of hate and calls down a curse on the Boards and the Martins of the earth, on all their servants, dupes, and followers:

'I will loose on them the blood of Christ!'

CHRIST HAS RETURNED from his forty-day stint in the desert, having resisted the blandishments of Satan.

He is standing in his father's workshop. The room and the objects it contains are so unfamiliar that he has no sense of a return. Has he ever used these adzes, saws, hammers, to make chairs and tables and cabinets?

There is a piece of rough timber in the vise. He picks up the adze. He knows this instrument is used to smooth and shape rough wood. For a moment he feels vibrations from the tool in his hand, fading like traces of a dream, leaving a dead weight in his fingers. He puts one hand on the wood and with the other delivers a sharp downward stroke aimed at a protruding knot.

The adze glances off the knot and cuts his

22

---

5. Remember the cave contains also all extinct diseases, the Seven Plagues of Egypt, the Hairs, the Pricks, the Sweats, all contained in the mold of man. Once the mold is shattered, all the plagues of time are released.

left hand between the thumb and forefinger. A deep cut, but he feels no more pain than if his hand itself were made of wood. He looks down in disbelief. The blood that drips out is not red but a pale yellow-green that gives off a reek of ammoniacal corruption, like rotten urine, the reek of man's sojourn on earth. Where the blood has fallen on the rough wood it eats in like acid, delineating a malignant simian face etched in hatred, evil, and despair.

With the fingers of his right hand he touches the wound, which knits and seals under his touch. Not even a scar remains.

AND A MAN came to Me with a sick monkey in his arms, and said: 'Heal my monkey.'

'I cannot heal animals, they have no soul.'

'They have grace and beauty and innocence. What are the people You heal but animals? Animals without grace, ugly animals deformed and diseased by the hate that has caused their sickness . . .' He cuddled his sick monkey and turned away. Then he looked back and said, 'Go heal Your lepers. And Your stinking beggars. Heal until You have nothing left to heal with.'

And others came with sick cats and ferrets. And one came with a sick child: 'This child has second sight. He can see what is in the mind of another. He can talk to the winds and the rain and the trees and the rivers. Heal him.'

'I cannot heal him because he knows not Me and he knows not Him who sent Me.'

'Then I care nothing for You, nor for Him who

sent You. For He sent You to make men less than they are, not more. He sent You to make slaves, not free men. He sent You to blind our eyes and stop our ears.'

THERE IS JUST so much energy, and every time I use it there is so much less. A woman sneaked up and touched My robe, and I said, 'Virtue has gone out of Me!' I could feel it go. It has a color and its color is blue, a deeper blue than the sea or the sky. I will use it all up and there will be no more, ever again.

Today a man came to Me. He said he was a painter and his eyes were failing. 'I do not ask to be healed for myself, but for the gift I have. I see what is behind faces and behind the hills and the trees and the sea. I see what no one else can see, and I paint what I see.'

I told him I could not heal him because he had no faith. He laughed, a hard, rasping sound like a file cutting bronze, and said: 'The people You heal are not worth healing. Is that why You heal them?'

'It is their faith that heals them.'

'That is a lie. I have painted a picture of You. It is a picture of a lie.' And he held the picture in front of My face. It was painted on a small square of some hardwood, and the colors followed the grain of the wood as if the wood had painted the picture.

I was startled because I had seen this face before, etched in wood where My blood had fallen when I cut Myself in My father's workshop. And there was a darkness in front of My eyes. When the darkness cleared, the man had gone.

*

MARINERS SAILING CLOSE to the coast of Tuscany heard a great voice speaking with the absolute certainty of words that will never again be heard.

'The great god Pan is dead!'

The date was December 25, year Zero A.D.[6]

AS MAGIC MEN in Morocco eat their excrement to distinguish themselves from other humans, Christ held power through the ancient corruption of a different blood. The question arises: Did Christ actually perpetrate the miracles attributed to him? My guess is that he did certainly commit some of these scandals. Buddhists consider miracles and healing dubious if not downright reprehensible. The miracle worker is

25

6. Miracles have to be paid for. Paid for in life, in beauty, in youth, innocence, joy, and hope . . . in the ephemeral moments. The magical moments . . . Little gray men play in his blockhouse at dawn, a little green reindeer floats in a green glade, the painter's light touches a red geranium in a Paris window box, catches a white cat on a red wall in Marrakesh. . . .

How much of this precious coinage did Christ borrow on human futures to heal one lousy idiot leper, one stinking, drooling, cross-eyed, harelipped beggar? Did Christ ever seek out a man who *deserved* to be healed because he had a special gift, a one-in-a-million talent? Unh-uh, Christ was concerned with quantity, not quality. From his standpoint it doesn't make any difference whom you heal. The point is to establish a monopoly *so no more miracles can ever occur.*

So Christ set out to destroy the raw material of miracles . . . souls, spirit, *djoun*, *prana*, the force that animates any living creature . . . spontaneous, unpredictable, alive. And what is Panic? The realization that everything is alive.

The great god Pan is dead.

upsetting the natural order, with incalculable long-range consequences, and is often motivated by self-glorification.

So, granted that Christ did work miracles, what he did was not so remarkable. Any competent magic man can heal (sometimes—can't win them all) and cast out devils, particularly if he installed them in the first place. Many practitioners can do weather magic. A few can raise the dead.

It was Christ's mission to demonstrate that these things could be done only once by one man or by some accredited representative. His mission was a lie. Christ set up a miracle monopoly and a monopoly on the medium of wonder.[7]

26   Christ called himself the Son of Man. I have said that Christ was the mold of man. This is not accurate; rather, he derived from the mold of man and

---

7. The teachings of Christ read like biological suicide. Shall the deer seek out the leopard and offer its throat to his fangs? Shall fish impale themselves on hooks and leap into nets? No animal species could survive by seeking out and loving its enemies. This is madness as practical advice, on a corporeal level. On a psychic level, if you can get that close to an enemy you can turn him into a friend, or kill him by alien proximity. A wise old magic man once told me: 'I have no enemies, I turn them all into friends.' He was the most deadly practitioner I have ever encountered.

The teachings of Christ make sense on a virus level. What does your virus do with enemies? It makes enemies into itself. If he hasn't caught it from the first cheek, turn the other cheek. There are few things more difficult than loving your enemies. So anyone who can do it will gain heavy power. Loving an enemy is an inhuman practice, placing the practitioner far above—or far below—the human level.

was the son of the mold. All species derive from molds. There are cat molds, deer molds, snake molds, centipede molds, primate molds. When the mold is destroyed or dies out, the species is extinct.

The unforgivable knowledge: *The Creator cannot create anymore* (if He ever could). He can only manipulate the creations of His mortal servants. It is slowly dawning on Him, as familiar objects emerge in the dawn's light, that He is being written off by Central Control.

His case officer once told him, in drunken confidence, that the most painful thing a case officer might have to do is write off a field agent. If the write-off is done expertly, the agent himself begins to doubt his mission and ultimately his sanity. Hearing voices? He can feel doom gathering, like a thick yellow fog, and feels the fear as his mission crumbles like shattered wood.

He begins to doubt that anyone has ever sent him, that he had any mission or purpose beyond the dictations of a disordered brain. Was there any Father who was sending him, speaking in his mind with a different voice? He has seen madmen shouting messages through the streets, bitten by dogs, stoned by children. Is he not just another lunatic clinging desperately to some absolute certainty, when his Truth is dust in the wind? The honorary agent of a planet that flickered out light-years ago . . .

Christ must have realized on the Cross that he had been set up. Without the Crucifixion, the whole deal is flat as last night's beer. So his ultimate mission was, by means of a potent symbol, to induce countless millions of human beings to accept a crippling lie. In fact, every man has the *potential* to heal and to influence the weather.

And the rationalists who reject his teachings are the most influential in perpetuating the lie. Between believers and non-believers, there is only a razor's edge; on both sides of the razor, the abyss of willful ignorance. None so blind as he who will not look.

Brion Gysin had the all-purpose nuclear bedtime story: Some trillions of years ago, a sloppy, dirty giant flicked grease from his fingers. One of those globs of grease is our universe, on its way to the floor.

Splat.

AFTER THE DEATH of Captain Mission, the blocked entrance of his adopted dwelling and the blasted tree that fronted it were protected by the Seven Guardians. The Guardians were not a hereditary order. When one Guardian died, the others sought out the replacement, who would be known by certain signs. Sometimes the chosen was an infant; in other cases an adolescent or an adult. Some of the elect were even quite elderly. Since there were only seven Guardians at one time, the order could maintain a high level of secrecy.

The land surrounding the tree and the

entrance was of course owned by the Guardians, and they had ways of discouraging intruders. Potential intruders, for some reason they could never formulate, turned by instinct away from the site. It was something to be forgotten as quickly as possible. So no one in the area even knew where the forbidden region was.

The Board knew about the Guardians but considered them laughable. They were convinced that Martin had effectively blocked the entrance, if there was an entrance. They did, however, dispatch agents to eliminate the Guardians and to appropriate the land. Three Guardians escaped, and the agents found no trace of the entrance.

The Board had indeed lost interest in what had come to be known as the Museum of Lost Species, some members even suggesting that the museum was a figment of the late Captain Mission's drug-clouded mind. In any case, there were more pressing matters: international dissent on an unprecedented scale. The Board's computers estimated that dissent would become acute in the next fifty to one hundred years. They had to think at least that far ahead.

To distract their charges from the problems of overpopulation, resource depletion, deforestation, pandemic pollution of water, land, and sky, they inaugurated a war against drugs. This provided a pretext to set up an international police apparatus designed to suppress dissidence on an international level.[8] The international apparatus was called ANA: Anti-Narcotics Association. In Arabic, *ana* means 'I,' so 'ANA' can be shortened to 'Eye.'

'ONE KOOK.'

'Yes, but . . . there are plenty who see through Eye right now.'

The Texas Board member looks up from his crossword puzzle.

'We should worry? We got the Moron Majority.'

'It's not a majority.'

'Who ever needed a majority? Ten percent plus the police and military is all it ever took. Besides, we've got the media, hook, line, and blinkers. Any big-circulation daily even hinting that the war against drugs is a red whale? Anyone asking why more money isn't going into research and treatment? Any investigative reporters looking into money laundering in Malaysia? Or the offshore bank accounts of Mahathir bin Mohamed? Anyone saying that the traffickers hanged in Malaysia are not exactly kingpins? There is no limit to what the media will swallow and spit out on their editorial pages. So?'

'But aren't we cutting our own lines?'

'No, just tightening up and eliminating small-time competition.'

8. As William von Raab of the U.S. Customs Service said: 'This is a war, and anyone who even suggests a tolerant attitude towards drug use should be considered a traitor.'

'But if we shoot all the addicts . . .'

'We won't. Just enough to put the price up, and there will of course be periods of lax enforcement.' So right out of the clear blue sky all the money on this money-built planet isn't even good for toilet paper.

And the ghost of Captain Mission nearly laughs himself solid: 'Going to try a new biologic agent, eh?'

III

IT WAS A clear day in Madagascar, perfect for burning, a brisk wind sweeping up the ravine to a stand of rain forest. A group of herdsmen were engaged in providing what they call 'a green bite' for their worthless zebus, a small black hump-backed breed of ox venerated by the natives and tied into some idiotic funerary practices.

A giant bulbous tree, its roots hugging the earth like a mother protecting her young, suddenly burst into a mass of flames, and there was a loud explosion, throwing stones and dirt into the air. (The explosion was occasioned by a powder keg left by Martin, one not detonated in the blast that had long ago sealed the entrance to the Museum of Lost Species.)

The herdsmen started back, protecting their

heads. No one was hurt. After some discussion, they decided someone attempting to blast away the tree had carelessly left some dynamite about.

Sifka Babirbutu was a man of some consequence, since he owned the largest herd of zebus in the district. When he arrived at his two-story house, a warm bath had already been prepared by his wife. After bathing, instead of putting on his usual linen pants and shirt, he selected his finest ceremonial gown.

His wife looked at him with cold disfavor.

'You drunk or something? Where's the funeral?'

'The funeral has come for all mankind unless they follow me. Nothing can save the world but the sacrifice of every zebu in Madagascar.'

His wife noticed a strange glow around his head and his voice, as she later reported to the man from the Disease Control Center: 'His voice went all through me. Then he gave a great cry that made my hair stand up like the quills on a tenrec, and fell dead as if struck by lightning.'

The victims of the disease that Sifka Babirbutu had contracted all shared, as autopsies later showed, a common abnormality: their veins were filled not with blood but with a yellow-green ichor that gave off a horrible stench. The disease spread with great rapidity to the African mainland, and from there to Europe and America.

In the first stage, the victims experienced

bizarre hallucinations and were convinced that they possessed miraculous powers, so that they rushed about putting their hands on anyone they found who was sick or crippled in any way. The afflicted were particularly troublesome in hospitals, rushing into operating rooms and delivery rooms. This stage was known to last for some hours, or days.

It was followed by a violent phase, in which the victim accused everyone in sight of betraying the Son of Man. And some, in their zealous dementia, were driven to release the fateful lightning of terrible, swift homemade flamethrowers and bizarre electrical devices, or to make bloody use of swords and axes. The terminal stage was grief, apathy, and death.[9]

34

THE VENERABLE SURGEON, with a sudden violent heave, dumps his patient off the operating table:

'Pick up your piles and walk. Don't want your type in here. Fucking *invalid*!'

The pastor sacrifices a human infant on the altar with a chain saw and quaffs a chalice of blood before his paralyzed flock can intervene.

---

9. As any astute physician well knows, the progress of disease according to the classic symptoms is more the exception than the rule. Any combination of the expected symptoms may be observed, or any corresponding lack of them. Sometimes, in the case of the Christ Sickness, the first symptom is death. In other cases the disease is insidious in its etiology and may take weeks or even months to manifest itself. In cases where the patient's vocation gives him a certain leeway, the disease may pass undetected until some outrageous lapse of duty has occurred.

It has been observed that police and military personnel start with the violent stage in full vigor, their destructive potential being limited only by a high incidence of cerebral hemorrhage.

IT IS ESTIMATED that a hundred million died of the Christ Sickness. But those who die are as nothing compared with the survivors.

'I am the way. None comes to the Father except through Me.'

Imagine hundreds of thousands of prophets, all saying with absolute conviction, *'I am the way,'* gathering disciples, even performing miracles. Special effects have come a long way since Jesus.

The Literalists—or 'Lits,' as they came to be known—actually put the words of Christ into disastrous practice.

Now Christ says if some son of a bitch takes half your clothes, give him the other half. Accordingly, Lits stalk the streets looking for muggers and strip themselves mother naked at the sight of one. Many unfortunate muggers were crushed under scrimmage pileups of half-naked Lits.

The Implacable Forgivers, a subset of Lits, will go to any lengths to seek out an enemy and forgive him. The Mafia don has barricaded himself in his Long Island retreat lest a rival don sneak in and collapse into his arms and forgive him all over for everything. Criminals storm the precincts, hands extended for the handcuffs. No doubt about it, brothers and sisters, love is the answer.

'Let love squirt out like a fire hose of molasses. Give him the kiss of life. Stick your tongue down his throat and taste what he has been eating and bless his digestion, *ooze* down into his intestines and help him along with his food. Let him know that you *revere* his rectum as part of an ineffable whole. Make him *know* that you stand in naked awe of his genitals as part of the Master Plan, life in all its rich variety.'

'Do not falter. Let your love enter in unto him and penetrate him with the Divine Lubricant, makes K-Y and lanolin feel like sandpaper. It's the most mucilaginous, the slimiest, ooziest lubricant ever was or shall be, amen.'

It's known as the Greasy Ghost, will love you all over and inside out. But there is folks say the Deadly Lovers is nothing but vile rotten vampires need a stake drove up the ass before they love us all down to a thick toothsome soup and slurp us all up. 'The Master Plan,' they call it.

THESE PRACTICES SOON precipitated an acute shortage of enemies, giving rise to Professional Enemy Services: PES. Just give us your specifications and our expert enemies will do the rest. Starting a new religion? Sect? No cult can make it without enemies. Where would Christianity be without the Crucifixion?

Need a personal enemy? Somebody special *just for you*? Well, mock up the consummate enemy,

everything you detest and everything that detests you, all the little mannerisms, details of dress, everything that rubs you the wrong way. Just feed your specifications into the computer and your personal enemy steps right out of the screen.

Love him or her, and you get your halo.

MEDUSA, WITH HER Afro hairdo of hissing snakes, raises a question: When does a halo become an extension, and how far can such extensions go? Eyes everywhere, in your TV set, your bedroom, your bathroom . . . bulbous red police noses sniffing for pot. Thousands of nosy brothers are smelling you, hearing you, watching you, 'round the clock. A mouth can undulate out on a sinuous pink tube to snap food from the plate or even the fork of an appalled gourmet, then retract, leaving a trail of intestinal slime.

Moreover, this Christ Sickness was only one of many plagues released by the fateful 'green bite' blast at the hidden door of the Museum of Lost Species, whose exhibits obviously included viruses as well as animals. As one viral strain burned itself out, or in rare instances when the scientists finally perfected a vaccine or a treatment, then another plague would take its place. Back to square one, Professor.[10]

*

10. Professor Unruh von Unerhört advanced a hypothesis that all the plagues were related, stemming from 'a basic and hideous flaw in ze origin of mankind. It is so coming home to ze rooster. Vat is needy is so an anti-*Menschen* serum.' The good professor's antiman

AND SO BACK to the zoological and botanical garden of extinct species. The Garden of Lost Chances. The sad streets of Lost Chance. Creatures too trusting and gentle to survive. A lemur frisks up to a bestial settler, who with an ugly snarl slashes it with his machete and leaves it to bleed to death.

'Try and bite me, will you. Fucking animals.'

And remember the passenger pigeons? Falling out of the trees like rain. You can sell all you can shoot. Good prices too.

The scenery here has a shattering impact, precipitous mountains, clefts and valleys falling away into lightless depths. It's all simultaneously present, the animals, plants, insects, invertebrates, amphibians, reptiles—all in their natural habitats. Tricky area coming up, the area of extinct diseases. Hungry after all these years.

Now, a disease usually becomes extinct because it has killed all available hosts and cannot find another in time. Many of these hotshot hundred-percent-fatal eager beavers don't last. They should get a little spread and stay there, like a cold or a cold sore or the humble wart. Some of them so deadly they'd wipe out a whole village in a week.

Fortunes of war. Plenty of good afflictions, hungry and waiting.

Here is the Hairs. Overnight a man's beard

---

serum proved fatal in a high percentage of cases, and quite useless in survivors, so it was soon abandoned.

has grown out to three inches and the Hairs is crawling all over him, heavy and rank, the roots reaching down into his stomach and intestines, closing around his liver and heart. In the end he'll look like a great bundle of hair.

NICK GRENELLI IS naturally hirsute, with black hair on his chest, back, and shoulders. He needs to shave twice a day.

One morning he wakes up to find his head hair over his ears and at least four days' growth of black beard on his face. The hair on his body and arms is also much longer, and there is a tingling sensation in his skin, as if he can *feel* the hairs growing. Shaken, he shaves and makes a cup of coffee.

Sitting down on the patio of his house in Miami, he notices that he has shed hairs from his forearms and the backs of his wrists onto the table, a film of fine black hairs, and then with a chill he notices that the hairs are moving, squirming like tiny living filaments, little black worms, in fact.

'My God!' he exclaims, and at that moment a gust of wind carries the hairs over the wall surrounding his patio, into the blue sky.

The following day, when he wakes up, there is a film of hair in front of his eyes, and as he moves in bed he can feel a cushion of hairs under his body. His nose is choked with hair, and his eyelashes and eyebrows cover his eyes. With a cry he rushes into the bathroom: his face is completely covered; great clusters of hair sprout from his ears, from the palms of his hands, from the bottoms of his feet. And the hairs are *alive*, all writhing and twisting with separate life. The hairs have grown through his cheeks and palate into his mouth and throat.

SUNDOWN SLIM WAKES up on a mattress on the traffic island that divides New York's Houston Street at the Bowery. He is seemingly covered by a fur coat. Sitting up groggily, he finds that the fur is under and not over his clothes, sprouting out through the openings of his shirt, from his ankles and his neck. He brushes hair out of his eyes.

'Well,' he decides, 'maybe I got the DTs.'

He feels in his watch pocket. A reassuring crinkle: two dollars. Enough for a quart of sherry. He lurches to his feet and makes his way across Houston and walks down the Bowery to a liquor store.

The proprietor looks at him with cold disfavor. 'Look, this isn't Halloween.'

'Huh?'

'What are you, the hairy ape?'

Slim puts his two dollars on the counter. But instead of picking up the money, the proprietor looks at the counter where hairs have fallen off Slim's hands and wrists and now twist, writhe, and jack-knife, long tendrils with white roots. The proprietor starts back with an exclamation of disgust.

'Get the fuck out of here and take your money with you!'

Bewildered, Slim lurches into the street. He feels a strange tingling sensation all over his body. Hairs are sprouting out of his fly. His nose is clogged with hairs. He can hardly breathe. People look at him and step aside. The hairs are *growing*. He begins tearing at his face and neck, and the hairs come out in tufts and drift away on a cold spring wind.

NICK GRENELLI CALLS his doctor. The doctor is shaken, but he tries to minimize the situation.

'They're alive, I tell you. Look!'

The doctor refuses to look.

'It's just differential elasticity. It's simply a glandular imbalance that can easily be corrected by the appropriate hormone supplements. You will have to come to the hospital for tests.'

The doctor has heard of other cases, but he has no idea as to treatment, if any. One case he recalls reading about concerned a woman who was covered with a sudden eruption of body hair. Hairs even grew from the palms of her hands and the soles of her feet.

The resident takes one look and orders Nick into isolation.

SLIM COLLAPSES ON a curb screaming, and as he screams the hairs billow out of his mouth and break away. Two cops approach, then stop.

'What the fuck? Hair growing all over him.'

'Better call an ambulance and stay away from him.'

41

'Hairs, you say?' A mutter of voices on the line.

'Listen. Don't touch him, but keep him in sight. We'll be there in three minutes.'

Sirens wailing, the ambulance pulls up. Men in coveralls with masks and goggles get out. They grab Slim with gloved hands and shove him into the ambulance. The cops look at the ambulance as it drives away, and shake their heads.

THE PROPRIETOR OF the liquor store looks at the squirming hairs on his counter.

'Some kinda worm, looks like.'

Suddenly one of the hairs jackknifes and fastens itself onto his thumb.

'Holy shit!' He jerks the hair out, but a little root remains embedded, and he feels a tingling sensation spreading from his thumb up his arm.

DOCTOR PIERCE WAKES from a nightmare. A huge hairy spider is on his face, suffocating him. Trembling, he turns on the light and goes into the bathroom. His face is covered in writhing hairs, with little barbed hooks at the ends. The phone rings. Overcome with horror, his voice muffled by hairs blocking his throat . . .

'Doctor Pierce?'

'Yes.'

'Doctor Mayfield here. You brought in a patient today? Nicola Grenelli?'

'Yes.'

'We've had a call from Atlanta. Seems he is suffering from a new disease and anyone who has come into contact with him is in danger of infection. I suggest you come in as soon as possible for tests.[11]

*

11. Consider the history of disease: it is as old as life. Soon as something gets alive, there is something there waiting to disease it. Put yourself in the virus's shoes, and wouldn't you do the same? How, when, and where did malaria start? They say AIDS is a simple variation on the visna virus, which occurs naturally in sheep and is always fatal. (Oh dear, have those sheepherders been naughty again?) And some say syphilis got its start from the fucking of a llama by a village idiot.

And the fearsome SEPs. Some organ of the body sets up shop and grows on its own: huge brains in fifty-five-gallon oil drums, a monster kidney that can be used for dialysis.

It's an ill fart that farts nobody any good.

The most dreaded SEP is the Pricks. Not a tumor, mind you, just a big prick and it keeps getting bigger. The smell, dank, rotten, and suffocating, is like something confined for centuries under a bell jar. The prick is already three feet long, and even as the victim looks, it is stirring and growing, lubricant oozing from the four slits at its head. The thing pulses with hideous need:

'Rub me! Rub me! Rub me!'

Moreover, the victim cannot keep his hand from rubbing lubricant around the tip of his prick. The thing ejaculates, immediately, throwing semen to the ceiling and twisting the victim's wasted body with wrenching spasms. He can feel tissue and bone dissolve, drawn into testicles big as baseballs. In the terminal stage the victim is reduced to a chrysalis attached to a huge penis; only his head remains, festooned with a necklace of pubic hairs.

Then there's airborne AIDS and the equally deadly Rejects, in which the immune system takes control of the body, rejecting first intestinal bacteria, then food itself, and finally the viscera, sloughing off one organ after another. Victims can be identified by their faces, frozen in a mask of rejection, and by a

43

MOVING ON: THE Red Spider Fever. The fever is transmitted by a small red spider about a quarter inch across. Within a few seconds of being bitten, the subject feels an intense burning itch at the site. The

---

graceless rigidity of bearing, as if they were made of glass. These victims isolate themselves in makeshift containers—boxes, tents, plastic sheets, multiple masks and gloves—all of which they constantly spray with disinfectant until they succumb to anorexia, dehydration, and internal stoppage.

These are also animal diseases: anthrax, aftosa, malignant distempers, and other viral illnesses. Starting in Madagascar, the cattle of the world were virtually annihilated. Sheep fared little better, decimated by a variation of the visna virus. Pigs and goats seemed more resistant, and for some reason wild species were comparatively immune. Dogs and cats, however, died by the millions, which was just as well, since there were no human owners left to feed and care for them.

No doubt cures and vaccines could have been found, except for the overwhelming caseload and consequent lack of time for even minimal care, let alone research, and, more crucial, the lack of qualified personnel to implement research. Scientists, technicians, computer programmers, mathematicians, and theorists have been virtually annihilated by a selective pestilence known as the Think Disease (or the Egg Heads).

The Think Disease is characterized by the isolation of the cerebral cortex from any motivation. So what does a computer do if there is no programmer to program it? Nothing. And that's what the victims of the Think Disease do, repeating the same formulas and theories over and over, like stuck records. Our weapon of choice against the virus is immunization . . . immunization . . . immunization . . . weapon weapon weapon . . . choice choice choice.

Without motivation . . . unable to carry out the simplest . . . dressing, eating . . . loll in their urine and excrement . . . must be spoon-fed . . . no time, no personnel for such a purpose . . . write them off along with catatonics and other terminals . . . no one to look after those who cannot or will not look after themselves . . .

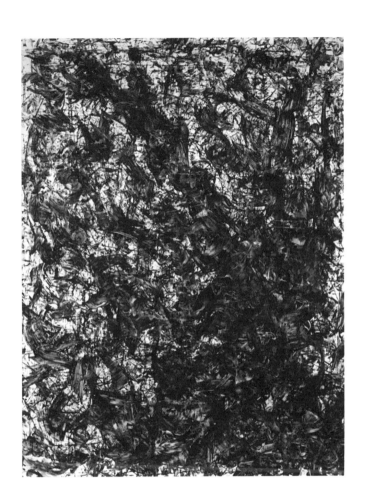

itch quickly spreads over the body until the subject feels his whole skin as one itching, burning, swelling hive. Glands in the armpits and groin swell and finally burst open as the patient, screaming in agony, experiences repeated involuntary orgasms and voids the bright red steaming excrement of the fever, from which spider eggs are already hatching. The disease then spreads to the internal organs, resulting in massive hemorrhages and suffocation from swelling in the throat and lungs. Death usually occurs within twenty-four hours of infection.

Geographically, the Red Spider Fever is confined to a small area, about ten miles long by a mile wide. Obviously there is something in this area essential to the life cycle of the spider. This locale, **45** known as the Redlands, also yields a metal that is like gold in appearance but far superior as an electrical conductor and harder than treated steel. The metal is as malleable as clay when mixed with certain solvents.

A six-month contract to mine in the Redlands and a man can live well for the rest of his life, so there are always candidates. But they must stick out the six months to get paid. Needless to say, the miners employ various repellents and methods of fumigation to circumvent the danger posed by the spider. The most reliable of these is an organic compound obtained by mixing gold salts with the coagulate of a red cactus indigenous to the area. Although this preparation, which can be injected or taken orally, is extremely addictive, it reduces the fever to a minor irritation, just as opium makes addicts immune to most respiratory infections.

The Goldies, as people using this medication are called, can easily be identified by a reflective golden sheen and receding deep-set gold-black eyes that shrink to round buttons. The ears grow close to the head and eventually sink into the flesh of it completely. Withdrawal symptoms are horrific, since the bones have been replaced by the gold salts, and if the gold is withdrawn the bones fracture and crumble from within; death occurs within twenty-four hours, with the victim in incredible agony. Aware of these side effects, many miners prefer to place their faith in rituals, incense, and less effective chemical repellents.

46

Repeated attempts have been made to exterminate the spiders, but the rocky desert soil provides hidden pockets where the spiders can wait out any pesticide program. The spiders have become immune to many agents, so alternative pesticides must be held in readiness for a dreaded mass attack.

The Redlanders live in cubicles cut into the red sandstone and gather nightly at the Gold Mine Bar. Some sip the Gold, others drink the Red Copper, an aphrodisiac potion that brings a user out in red hives like a mild case of the fever. The Red Copper conveys a limited immunity to the fever but is ineffectual against multiple bites. Nobody has ever been bitten in the Gold Mine Bar.

*

THE EXTINCT DISEASES, my dear, some of them can kill in *minutes*. Ravenous diseases lurk in dust and straw, mist and swamps and fossilized rock. Some of the deadliest are parasite plants specialized to grow in human flesh, like the Roots. Roots grow down into the viscera and glands, curling around bones; vines sprout from the victim's groin and armpits; green shoots spring from his penis tip; tendrils creep out of his nostrils to release deadly seeds that then spread on the wind; thorns tear out his eyes; his testicles swell and burst with roots; his skull becomes a flowerpot for stunning brain orchids that grow over dead eyes and idiot face while the skin slowly toughens into bark. In some cases metamorphosis is complete. The subject grows into the ground to know the exquisite agony of quickening sap, of leaves eating light and roots nourished by water, shit, and soil.

47

Other subjects are invaded by a plant like a Venus's-flytrap that breaks through pustules all over the body to eat the swarms of insects drawn to the sweet gum exuded by the plant . . . fat june bugs, grasshoppers, caterpillars, bees, wasps, hornets.[12]

*

12. In Madagascar there was at one time a man-eating plant, eight feet high and three feet in diameter, with a bulbous green-purple stomach. Tentacles with sticky spines would protrude from the top of the plant to seize and hold its prey as a poisonous juice immobilized the unlucky victim.

According to an early traveler, the natives feared and worshiped this plant, which had the ability to project its hunger in a way they could not resist. So they developed the practice of

THE STREETS OF Lost Chance. Man knows he has one chance in a million to make the connection that will animate the creature he carries in his body. If he doesn't make it, the little creature will die inside him. The pressure makes him utterly ruthless. Anything to protect the child. He can lie, pretend, kill without a second's qualm. For he is the bearer, the guardian of the one child in a million.

There were of course species that became extinct before man, but Homo Sap added a twist. He has killed to eat, but he has also killed for pleasure, to be sure. Moreover, he has killed for the sheer ugliness of the thing. The Thing inside him. The Ugly Spirit who found a worthy vessel in Homo Sap, the Ugly Animal.

What else distinguishes Homo Sap from other animals? He can make information available through writing or oral tradition to other Sap humans outside his area of contact and to future generations. This distinction led Count Korzybski to call man 'a time-binding animal,' and it can be reduced to one word: *language* . . . the representation of an object or process by symbols, signs, sounds—that is, by *something it is not*. Korzybski would begin a lecture by thumping on a desk and saying, 'Whatever this may

---

sacrificing captives to the organism. When a captive was brought to the plant, the tentacles would twist and writhe, giving off such vile odors, the observer reported, that he was unable to eat for ten days afterward.

be, it *is not* a desk or table.' That is, the object is not the label.

Man sold his soul for time, language, tools, weapons, and dominance. And to make sure he doesn't get out of line, these invaders keep an occupying garrison in his nondominant brain hemisphere. How else to explain anything as biologically disadvantageous as a weak hand? They gave with one hand and took back with the other. Fifty-fifty. What could be fairer than that? Almost anything.

So it seems likely that the distinguishing factors, language and weak hand, are related. It seems unlikely that language was designed solely to convey information.

A rift is built into the human organism, the rift or cleft between the two hemispheres, so any attempt at synthesis must remain unrealizable in human terms. I draw a parallel between this rift separating the two sides of the human body and the rift that divided Madagascar from the mainland of Africa. One side of the rift drifted into enchanted timeless innocence. The other moved inexorably toward language, time, tool use, weapon use, war, exploitation, and slavery.

It would seem that merging the two is not viable, and one is tempted to say, as Brion Gysin did, *'Rub out the word.'*

But perhaps 'rub' is the wrong word. The formula is quite simple: reverse the magnetic field so that, instead of being welded together, the two halves repel each other like opposing magnets. This could be a road to final liberation, as it were, a final solution to the language problem, from which all human 'problems' stem.

What would a wordless world be like? As Korzybski said: 'I don't know. Let's see.'

Nothing is more expensive than to change the dies, the *molds*, and that is why the Boards and Syndicates and their subsidiary politicians, mafias, drug agents, police, churches, and news media don't want to know about a better human product, any more than General Motors wants to know about a turbine engine. It would mean scrapping all existing dies from here to eternity.

50   And that is why dissent is of such concern to the Board: if diverted from its usual political expression, *dissent could shatter the hallowed mold*. Political dissent most often turns into whatever it opposes. America is turning into Stalinist Russia, becoming a complete control state with zero tolerance for dissent on any level.

THERE WAS ONCE a period of rampant hybridization, which gave rise to the variety of species we see today. We can observe in fact a number of transitional creatures, such as the jaguarundi, which is classified as a cat but looks more like an arboreal otter. But the majority of the hybrids did not survive, and those that did survive erected a rigid biological defense against any further hybridization.

What destroyed most of the hybrids, especially the really bizarre models? They were all attacked and killed by a series of virulent plagues. For hybridization to occur, there must be suppression of the immune reaction. This gave disease its opening. Disease frightened the survivors into immutable biological molds.

THE MUSEUM OF Lost Species is not exactly a museum, since all of the species are alive in dioramas of their natural habitats. Admission is free to anyone who can enter. The coinage here is the ability to endure the pain and sadness of observing extinction and by so doing to reanimate the species by observing it.

Consider some of the extinct species: creatures that eat grass or flesh with equal relish, humanoid bats with luminous wings, warm-blooded reptiles capable of mammalian affection (a beautiful green snake nuzzles at my face), cold-blooded carrion birds, romping turtles and lizards affectionate as puppies, a hybrid of lemur and octopus that lives in the lakes and rivers of Madagascar, changing color with every shift and nuance of feeling.

Or take the humanoid albino lemur, with enormous disklike eyes of a nacreous silver and huge ears that tremble and vibrate to every sound. The eyes are without pupils, their vision as if they saw through a very wide-angle lens without focus. The creature is not without defenses, being equipped with strong needle claws and sharp canines. Like all albinos, they are also extremely delicate. Weighing about fifty pounds at maturity, they are arboreal and semiaquatic. Naturally, as albinos, they are unable to tolerate light. During the daytime they hide in caves or in retreats under riverbanks.

A plant man who grows from one place to another, festooned with lethal orchids and stinging vines; an electric-eel man, six feet of sleek brown-purple with mud-cool green-brown eyes: both hermaphroditic, fertilizing themselves and giving birth . . . A vegetable consciousness that moves through the forest, feeling its way into trees and vines and orchids, and looks like a green jellyfish floating in a green medium . . . A dog creature with a vine tail and thorn teeth . . . Intelligent birds, of a light porous texture, like sponges . . . They have large brains, enormous eyes, very small bodies, and long retractable talons. They eat fruit and fish, which they can spot at a great distance with their keen vision. Their digestive system will not process fur, so they do not prey on mammals or other birds.

The Root People, to give another example, have circumvented the basic disadvantage of the vegetable kind: they take nourishment from plants and trees, and move from one to another, careful not to overstay their welcome. They can burrow under the earth like moles, putting up a hand or popping out a head to test the weather and other factors. Caught in a desert area, they put down long taproots and then surface long enough to gather solar energy before tunneling out of the area.

The Green People have found a way to nourish themselves through photosynthesis, converging in calm green swirls and eddies. Some take to water, develop gills, and live on algae. Some nourish themselves on odors, which they breathe in through pores that they can open to the size of a match head. Others eat light and color so that their bodies finally melt into light.

NO WAY TO know how many die of the plagues. In fact, starvation, exposure, violence, and the old standbys pneumonia, tetanus, dysentery, cholera, diphtheria, typhoid, scarlet fever, hepatitis, TB, untreated VD, and general infections take as high a toll as all the Plagues of Mad, as they are called.

Warlords spring up. Prophets who have survived the Christ sickness gain followers and declare Holy War on other prophets and the unconverted populace at large—'Ye assholes of little faith'—killing anyone they come across. Cannibalism is rampant.

Crusades against the Infidels are proposed but cannot be implemented since the Western world is split into thousands of factions, each in deadly opposition to the others. Despite pandemic paranoia, atomic weapons have not been used since 1945: anyone who could have implemented them has already died from overthinking. Even a sick wind can blow good.

The research scientists lived in fortified compounds guarded by what remained of the military and police. However, the scientists found themselves under heavy incentive to produce.

'Well, boys, we got just fourteen days to come up with a serum or a cure for the Hairs, or else . . .'

Whenever time ran out, a lethal gas was released in the laboratory. All the labs were separate and hermetically sealed. So that was that. A salutary lesson to the survivors.

Outside the compounds, total chaos reigned as the plagues raged unchecked, and all pretense of law and order had long since been abandoned. The country was dotted by fortresses, to ward off foraging bands from the starving cities.

And what happened to the Board? They have retreated to their yachts and islands and bunkers. Their power, which depended on manipulation through money and political contacts, is gone.

The Four Horsemen ride through ruined cities and neglected, weed-grown farms. The virus is burning itself out, its victims dying by the millions.

People of the world are at last returning to their source in spirit, back to the little lemur people of the trees and the leaves, the streams, the rocks, and the sky. Soon, all sign, all memory of the wars and the Plague of Mad will fade like dream traces.

Afterword

THE FIRST NAME of the libertarian, pirate Captain Mission, or Misson, is lost to history. All that we know of Mission comes from the book *A General History of the Most Notorious Pirates*, published in London in 1724 and written by one Captain Charles Johnson (although there is a current of thought that attributes the work to Defoe). The memoirs of Mission, handwritten in French, were apparently saved by a member of the crew who survived Mission's last voyage, and after passing through several hands they were translated by Johnson and included in his book.

Mission came from a wealthy Provençal family, and studied humanities, logic, and mathematics at the university of Angers in the late seventeenth century. His first commission was a French man-o'-

war, the *Victoire*, mounting thirty guns and commanded by a distant cousin. The ship sailed first to Naples, and Mission traveled to Rome, where he met a young priest named Caraccioli. While Mission was making his confession, he was surprised to discover the priest shared his own disgust for the hypocrisy of earthly power, temporal and spiritual. Caraccioli threw off his frock and signed onto the *Victoire*.

The frigate engaged and defeated two Algerian vessels, Caraccioli receiving a thigh wound. Other engagements were also successful. The *Victoire* crossed the Atlantic, and off Martinique in the Caribbean it was set upon by the English *Winchelsea*, commanded by Captain Opium Jones. The first broadside killed the *Victoire*'s captain, second captain, and three lieutenants, whereupon Mission commanded the men, with Caraccioli at his side, and they repulsed the English. Mission was named captain by the whole crew, and for their pirate flag they raised a white ensign with LIBERTÉ painted on it.

After many other adventures on the coast of West Africa, and joined now by a captured English ship and crew, Mission helped the queen of Johanna wage war on neighboring Mohilla, both islands lying between Mozambique and the great red island, Madagascar. He and his men took a Portuguese ship and decided to settle permanently on Madagascar. Here, around 1700, at a remote harbor at the north end of the island, Mission built two great octagonal forts, and with his band of several hundred French and

English pirates, renegade seamen, and freed slaves he established the free colony of Libertatia.

Together with his lieutenant Caraccioli and the converted English pirate-captain Thomas Tew, Mission formulated a set of Articles by which the settlement might live in peaceful democracy. These Articles were based on ideas remarkably like the ideas behind the French and American revolution of the late eighteenth century—and preceded them by more than sixty years. There would be no capital punishment, no slavery, no imprisonment for debt, and no interference with religion or sexuality. Caraccioli divided the men into groups of ten, called states, and the position of lord conservator was established, as well as an annual plenary meeting. The first meeting lasted ten days. Tew was made admiral, Caraccioli secretary of state, and Mission became His Supreme Excellence the Lord Conservator.

57

On a cruise off southern Madagascar, Captain Tew and some English sailors he had recruited drank rum punch too late into the last night of the journey, and the tide carried the noble *Victoire* out to sea, where she cracked apart on the rocks. The crew was lost, and Tew pitched a makeshift camp and waited to be rescued.

While Captain Tew waited at his lonely, distant cove, two huge bands of Malagasy natives swept down upon Libertatia in the dead of night and wiped out the colony. Caraccioli died in this attack, and Mission escaped with only forty-five men and two sloops. In time he found his way to Captain Tew's remote harbor, and the two men decided to retire to America, where they were both unknown. In a great storm off Cape Infanta, their sloop was lost beneath the waves.[13]

13. Today it is the lemurs of Madagascar that are threatened with extinction. When humans first arrived on the island, fifteen hundred years ago, there were some forty species; now only twenty-two remain, and all are considered endangered. In some parts of the island the natives hunt slow lemurs for their meat, although in other places they are protected by a taboo. The human population is growing rapidly and may reach twelve million by the year 2000; meanwhile the ongoing deforestation and slash-and-burn agriculture have destroyed ninety percent of the original forests, the lemurs' natural habitat. It is projected that the lemurs of Madagascar may be gone in a hundred years, the legacy of one hundred sixty million years destroyed in our lifetime.

In an 83-acre forest near Durham, North Carolina, the Duke University Primate Center maintains a colony of more than six hundred prosimians, mostly lemurs, some of them in semi-wild natural enclosures. This colony was started at Yale in 1958 and moved to Duke in 1968. When a ruffed lemur gave birth in that year, it was the first lemur birth in captivity anywhere in forty years. More than three hundred lemurs have been born at the Primate Center since then. Director Elwyn L. Simons has established good relations with the Malagasy government and was able to bring nine wild-caught sifakas to the Duke compound in 1987.

The Duke University Primate Center needs financial support from concerned individuals. Write to DUPC, Duke University, Durham, North Carolina 27706.

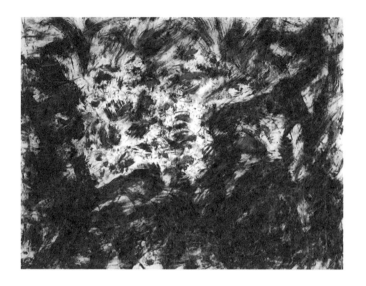